SYDNEY & TAYLOR
Take a Flying Leap

JACQUELINE DAVIES

Illustrated by **DEBORAH HOCKING**

Houghton Mifflin Harcourt
Boston   New York

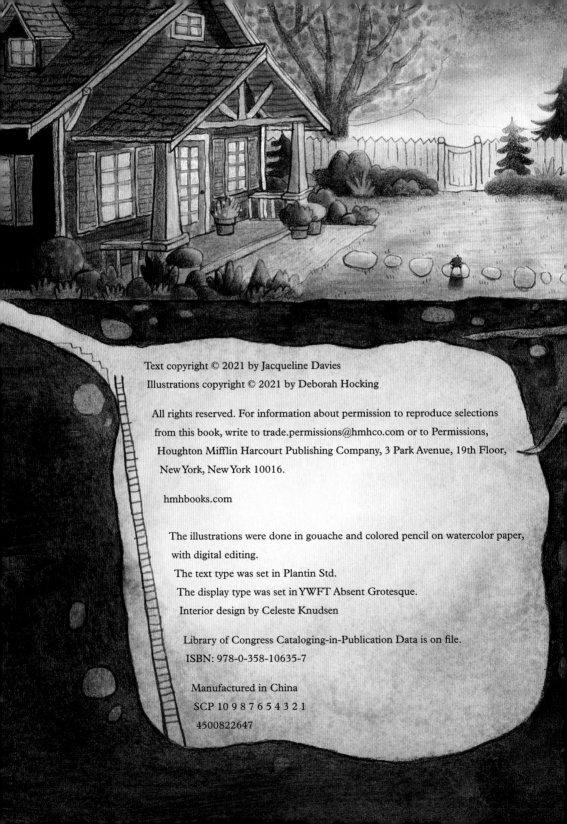

Text copyright © 2021 by Jacqueline Davies

Illustrations copyright © 2021 by Deborah Hocking

All rights reserved. For information about permission to reproduce selections from this book, write to trade.permissions@hmhco.com or to Permissions, Houghton Mifflin Harcourt Publishing Company, 3 Park Avenue, 19th Floor, New York, New York 10016.

hmhbooks.com

The illustrations were done in gouache and colored pencil on watercolor paper, with digital editing.

The text type was set in Plantin Std.

The display type was set in YWFT Absent Grotesque.

Interior design by Celeste Knudsen

Library of Congress Cataloging-in-Publication Data is on file.

ISBN: 978-0-358-10635-7

Manufactured in China

SCP 10 9 8 7 6 5 4 3 2 1

4500822647

*To those who are brave enough to leap and to the loyal
friends they land on — J.D.*

*For Summer: adventurer, dreamer,
best friend forever — D.H.*

Chapter 1

Sydney was dreaming.

In his dream, he wandered through the Backyard. Every few steps he found a tuna fish sandwich!

It was a wonderful dream.

Then the sandwiches began to whisper his name. *Sydney,* they whispered. *Sydney . . . Sydney . . .*

"Sydney!" a voice shouted.

Sydney jumped.

Oh! It was Taylor!

Sydney and Taylor lived in a burrow under Miss Nancy's potting shed. The burrow was cozy. The burrow was quiet.

That's exactly how Sydney liked it.

"I have a Big Idea!" shouted Taylor.

Sydney sighed. "You had a Big Idea on Thursday. You had a Big Idea on Friday. Today is Saturday. Can you ignore this Big Idea for the weekend?" asked Sydney.

Taylor tried.

He looked at the ceiling.

He looked at the floor.

He looked at his paws and his belly and the tip of his nose.

"No!" he said. "A Big Idea cannot be ignored."

"Okay," said Sydney. "Let's hear it."

"Come outside," said Taylor.

Sydney and Taylor climbed out of the burrow.

Sydney breathed in the fresh air. It was wonderful.

"Look up!" said Taylor.

Sydney looked up. A circle of birds flew overhead.

"My Big Idea is—" said Taylor. He was so excited he hopped from one foot to the other.

"I am going to fly!"

Chapter 2

"What?" asked Sydney.

"Fly!" said Taylor. "Like a bird! I will finally see the Whole Wide World!"

Sydney tried not to laugh. He covered his mouth. He scrunched his toes. He even bit the tip of his tongue.

But it was no use. Sydney laughed so hard he accidentally squirted some musk.

Taylor stamped his foot. "You are not being a good friend!"

"I'm sorry, Taylor!" said Sydney, gasping for air. "It's just that—a *flying hedgehog?*" Sydney fell to the ground, laughing.

"Other animals fly!" said Taylor.

"Yes," said Sydney, "but other animals have wings."

"Then I will get wings!" said Taylor. "I will make them. Or find them. Or borrow them."

"Wings are not something you can make or find or borrow," said Sydney. "You must be born with wings."

Taylor glared at Sydney. "A *friend* would help another friend fly," said Taylor. "I am going to fly all by myself!"

Taylor stomped off.

Sydney was loyal, as all skunks are. He helped Taylor with his Big Ideas, no matter how silly they were. But this Big Idea was impossible. Hedgehogs could not fly.

Chapter 3

"Excuse me, Birds?" squeaked Taylor. He was standing in the middle of the Backyard.

Normally, Taylor was afraid of animals he didn't know. But this was a Big Idea, and he needed help. He straightened his spine and shouted, "Birds?"

One of the birds landed nearby.

"Can you carry me in the air?" asked Taylor.

"*Trill!* You are too heavy," said the bird. "The only one who can—*trill!*—carry you is the Great Hawk. And you don't want *that.*"

The Great Hawk was a Ferocious Predator. She would eat Taylor if she had the chance!

Just thinking about the
Great Hawk made Taylor's spine curl.
When hedgehogs are frightened,
they curl up into a tight ball.

Buzz. Buzz. Buzz.

"What is that noise?" asked Taylor.

The bird ruffled her feathers. "It is the
Boy," she said. "He has a new toy."

The Boy lived next door to Miss Nancy.

He was noisy. He was messy. He was careless.

Sometimes he shouted for no reason.

Sometimes he stepped on Miss Nancy's flowers.

Sometimes he threw things over the fence. It was hard to be a small animal when unexpected things came flying over the fence.

"I might—*trill! trill!*—carry you with the help of friends," said the bird. "Go find a blanket and meet me here." She flew away.

When Taylor returned to the burrow, Sydney said, "I will *not* let you take a blanket. This is a dangerous Big Idea."

So Taylor grabbed his own blanket

and hurried outside.

He couldn't wait to fly!

Chapter 4

The bird and her friends were waiting in the Backyard.

"Sit in the middle," the bird told Taylor.

Flap, flap, flap!

Taylor felt the blanket begin to rise. He looked over the edge.

"Come down!" shouted Sydney.

Just then, a swarm of flies appeared.

"Lunchtime!" crowed the birds.

They chased the flies, but they did
not let go of the blanket. The blanket
began to tear.

"Yipes!" cried Taylor, holding tight.

"Hang on, Taylor!" shouted Sydney.

"I will catch you!"

Taylor fell

and fell

and fell.

Crash!

"You *landed* on me!" said Sydney.

"You *stood* under me!" said Taylor.

Taylor tried to get up. But he didn't know which way was up. He didn't know which way was down. He was so dizzy, he fell over.

He lay on his back, staring at the sky.

"Oh, Taylor," said Sydney. "Now do you see that hedgehogs can't fly?"

"I do not see that *at all*. I see the big, blue sky." Taylor stood up. "And I am going to fly up there!"

Chapter 5

Taylor walked to the edge of the Backyard,

where he found a deer nibbling on a dandelion.

"Excuse me," said Taylor.

The deer looked up. "Do I know you?"

"No," said Taylor. "But I need some *big* help.

And you are a very big animal."

"What kind of help?" asked the deer.

"I want to fly," said Taylor.

The deer looked at Taylor carefully. She

walked in a circle around him.

"You are *round*," said the deer. "You are *heavy*. And you do not have *wings*."

Taylor nodded his head. "I know!" He almost began to cry.

The deer nibbled on another dandelion and thought. "What we need," she said, "is a flying expert."

"A bird?" asked Taylor. "I tried that."

"No," said the deer. "You are a mammal, not a bird. We need a mammal who flies."

Far away, they heard a *buzz*.

"There's that noise again," said Taylor.

"The Boy," said the deer. "He has a new toy. It will probably come crashing over the fence any minute."

Taylor and the deer looked at the fence.

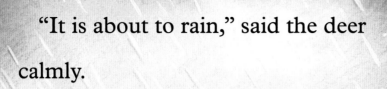

"It is about to rain," said the deer calmly.

She climbed delicately onto the back porch just as the sky cracked open and rain poured down.

Taylor scrambled onto the back porch.

A bat swooped in. "Wow! Some rain!" she said. She spread her wings to dry.

"Your wings are *beautiful*," said Taylor.

The deer looked at the bat's wings. "Your wings have delicate bones, thin webbing, and a scalloped edge."

The bat flapped her strong wings to shake off the water. Taylor stepped back and knocked over an umbrella. The umbrella snapped open.

The bat, the deer, and Taylor all stared at the umbrella.

Chapter 6

It was hard to walk with his new wings. They dragged on the ground.

A crowd of animals gathered. Taylor looked for Sydney, but didn't see him.

"You don't look like a bat," said a squirrel.

"I don't feel like one, either," said Taylor.

The deer pulled on the rope that lifted Taylor up, up, up. The ground was very far away. His wings felt strange.

"Excuse me?" Taylor asked the bat. "How *exactly* do you fly?"

"It's easy!" said the bat. "Watch!" She dipped and soared, zipped and zoomed. "See?"

Taylor did *not* see. He trembled on the edge of the roof. *Oh! How I wish Sydney was here,* he thought.

And just then, he heard Sydney's voice!

"Taylor! Get down off that roof!"

"*Now?*" shouted Taylor in a panic. "I don't think I'm quite ready!"

"No!" said Sydney, stamping his foot. "I mean let me lower you safely with the rope. Hedgehogs *cannot* fly."

"But I have wings," said Taylor. "Just like a bat!"

Sydney shook his head.

"Taylor. Your wings are not like a bat's. Your wings are like an umbrella."

Suddenly, Taylor realized how much danger

he was in. He was frightened.

Snap!

His body became a tight ball.

Taylor rolled off the roof.

Chapter 7

"Sydney!" shouted Taylor as he fell

through the air.

Sydney ran to catch him.

Taylor tried to flap his wings.

He spiraled like a helicopter

out of control.

Crash! Taylor landed on Sydney.

"*Twice!* In one day!" said Sydney. "But I am glad you are not hurt."

"I *am* hurt," wailed Taylor.

"Where?" asked Sydney.

"*Here,*" said Taylor, pointing to his heart. "In all the years we've been friends, you have *always* helped me with my Big Ideas. Even when they were silly."

Sydney looked at his dear friend. "Taylor," he said, "hedgehogs *cannot fly.*"

"I know," said Taylor. "I just thought . . . it was such a wonderful Big Idea. I guess some ideas are *too* big."

Buzz, buzz, buzz. Suddenly, it sounded as if a swarm of bees was heading straight for the Backyard.

A noisy toy came flying over the fence, crashed into the Big Oak Tree, and landed in a pile of leaves.

Sydney and Taylor stared at it.

They sniffed it. It smelled of the Boy.

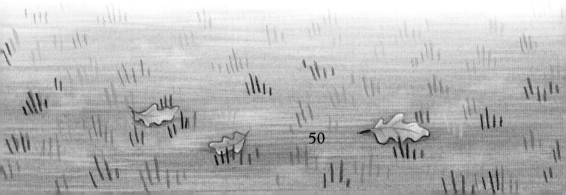

Just then, they heard Miss Nancy and the Boy talking. They heard footsteps coming toward the Backyard.

"Quick!" shouted Sydney. "Cover the toy with leaves!"

"Why?" asked Taylor.

"Because," said Sydney, "there's no such thing as a Big Idea that is too big."

Chapter 8

The Boy glanced around the Backyard, then he shrugged. "I guess it landed somewhere else."

Sydney and Taylor did not know what the Boy was saying. They were Wild Animals and did not understand the Language of Humans.

The Boy put something down on the
porch and picked up the umbrella. "Hey,
can I have this?" he asked.

Miss Nancy nodded. She looked at the
broken umbrella, then stared at the potting
shed.

"Can you give me a ride to the hardware
store?" asked the Boy.

A moment later, Sydney and Taylor heard

Miss Nancy and the Boy drive away.

Then Sydney saw something on the porch.

"Look," whispered Sydney.

The Boy had left a plastic box.

"What is it?" asked Taylor.

"I don't know what it *is*," said Sydney, "but

I bet I know what it *does*."

Chapter 9

"I can't believe I'm going to *fly!*" shouted Taylor.

Sydney had practiced flying the toy over and over. *Just in case.*

Taylor had made a special helmet out of a walnut shell. *Just in case.*

The birds had given feathers to Taylor. *Just in case.*

"Ready, Taylor?" shouted Sydney.

"Ready, Sydney!" yelled Taylor.

"Here we go!" Sydney pushed a
button.

Slowly, the toy lifted off the ground. All the animals cheered.

"I'm flying, Sydney!" shouted Taylor.

"You sure are, Taylor!"

Taylor and the toy circled the yard once. Sydney was very careful with the levers. He knew his friend's life depended on him.

"Just one more time around, Taylor," said

Sydney. Soon it would begin to get dark, and

Miss Nancy and the Boy would return.

Taylor felt the breeze blowing on his face. He could see all of the Backyard and even the Whole Wide World beyond. There were mountains and valleys and rivers and forests. Taylor could see them for *real,* not just on his map. For the first time in his life, Taylor felt BIG.

Sydney pushed gently on one lever. The toy began to fly lower.

But when he pressed on the right lever, it got stuck! Sydney pushed and pushed, but the lever wouldn't move. Taylor and the toy began to rise.

"Taylor," he called, "we have a problem!"

"I can see that!" shouted Taylor. The toy was headed straight for the Big Oak Tree.

"Prepare for a crash landing!" yelled Sydney.

Snap!

Taylor rolled into a tight ball.

Crash!

He slammed into the Big Oak Tree.

Taylor opened his eyes. He was

dangling twenty feet above the ground.

But that was not Taylor's biggest

problem.

A shadow passed over him.

The Great Hawk had spotted him,

and she was hunting for dinner.

Chapter 10

"Don't be afraid, Taylor!" shouted Sydney. "I'm coming!"

"I'm not afraid, Sydney!" shouted Taylor, trying to be brave. The Great Hawk swooped closer.

Taylor knew that skunks were poor climbers. Their claws were too long. He would have to rescue himself. He needed a Big Idea. Right now!

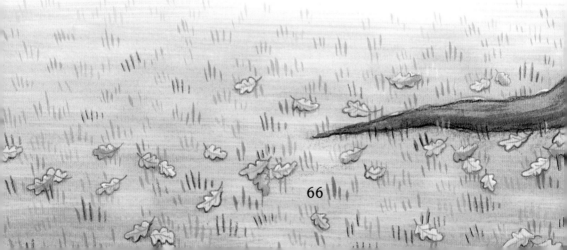

The Great Hawk landed on the branch

next to Taylor.

"What *are* you?" she asked.

Taylor puffed out his chest. "I . . . I . . .

I am a Scary Predasaurus!" he said loudly.

"You look like a tiny hedgehog covered in bird feathers," said the Great Hawk. "But lucky for you, there is bigger prey nearby." She looked down at Sydney, who was trying to climb the tree.

"You can't eat *Sydney!*" said Taylor. "He's a stinky skunk."

The Great Hawk flapped her wings. "Hawks have no sense of smell. We eat *everything.*" And then off she flew.

Chapter 11

"Run, Sydney! Run!" shouted Taylor. "The Great Hawk is after *you!*"

"Crispy crickets!" shouted Sydney when he looked up and saw the hawk circling above.

His only chance was to make a dash for the
burrow.

But he couldn't leave Taylor.

The Great Hawk swooped closer.

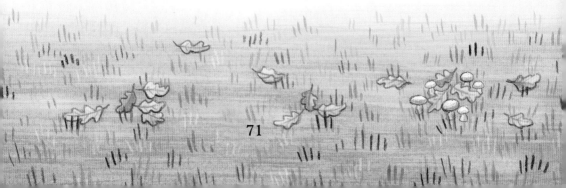

Taylor began to jump up and down on the broken toy. He grabbed it with all four paws and began to rock back and forth. "I have a Big Idea, Sydney!"

He pushed and pulled and rocked and rolled and jumped and stamped—until the toy fell out of the tree.

Three of the propellers began to buzz. One of the legs fell off. Taylor's feathers fluttered away.

"ROAR!" shouted Taylor as he steered

the toy by leaning this way and that.

"*SCREECH!*" yelled the Great Hawk.

The Great Hawk flew far away from the
Scary Predasaurus who landed with a bump
on the ground.

Chapter 12

Sydney brushed away the crumbs from his tuna fish sandwich. Taylor was still thinking about his glorious flight.

He had been the world's first flying hedgehog, and he had saved his friend's life. He would never feel small again.

"Someday we will write a story about this Big Idea," said Taylor.

"Maybe we will, Taylor," said Sydney, already settling in for a nap. "But for now, let's just be glad we're both alive. And that we have our cozy burrow. And that we have each other."

"Yes," said Taylor. He closed his eyes, too. He could hardly wait for his next Big Idea to arrive.

Continue to explore with:

Best-selling author of the Lemonade War series
Jacqueline Davies

SYDNEY & TAYLOR

EXPLORE the Whole Wide World

Illustrated by **Deborah Hocking**

★ " With a nod to *The Wind in the Willows* (not to mention that wink to the author of the All-of-a-Kind Family books), Davies sends an odd-couple pair of animal burrow mates out to explore the 'whole wide world.' Hocking illustrates the short chapters with delicately detailed scenes of settled, peaceful countryside and cozy subterranean digs."

— *Booklist,* (starred review)

And don't miss:

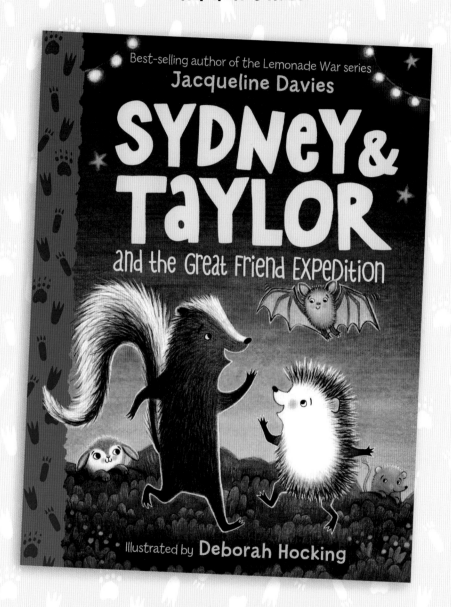

Best-selling author of the Lemonade War series
Jacqueline Davies

SYDNEY & TAYLOR
and the Great Friend Expedition

Illustrated by **Deborah Hocking**

Coming in Feb. 2022

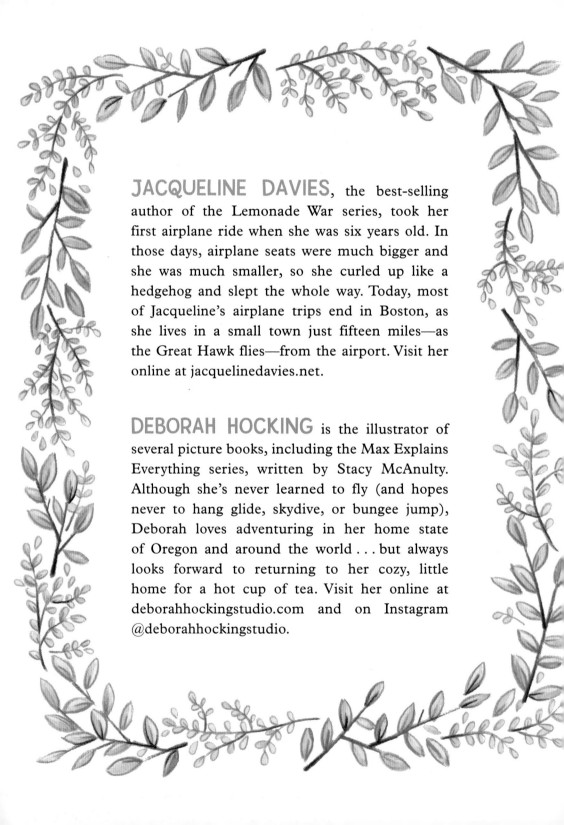

JACQUELINE DAVIES, the best-selling author of the Lemonade War series, took her first airplane ride when she was six years old. In those days, airplane seats were much bigger and she was much smaller, so she curled up like a hedgehog and slept the whole way. Today, most of Jacqueline's airplane trips end in Boston, as she lives in a small town just fifteen miles—as the Great Hawk flies—from the airport. Visit her online at jacquelinedavies.net.

DEBORAH HOCKING is the illustrator of several picture books, including the Max Explains Everything series, written by Stacy McAnulty. Although she's never learned to fly (and hopes never to hang glide, skydive, or bungee jump), Deborah loves adventuring in her home state of Oregon and around the world . . . but always looks forward to returning to her cozy, little home for a hot cup of tea. Visit her online at deborahhockingstudio.com and on Instagram @deborahhockingstudio.

THE WHOLE

OLD FOOTBRIDGE